Mr. Bear Babysits

by Debi Gliori

An Artists & Writers Guild Book

Golden Books
Western Publishing Company, Inc.

for Leslie Gardiner
my dear friend
with lots of love

First published in Great Britain in 1994 by Orchard Books.

Library of Congress Cataloging-in-Publication Data
Gliori, Debi.
Mr. Bear babysits/by Debi Gliori.
p.   cm.
Summary: The young Grizzly-Bears try the patience of a new babysitter.
$13.95
[1. Babysitters—Fiction. 2. Bears—Fiction.]
I. Title. II. Title: Mister Bear babysits.
PZ7.G4889Mr 1994   [E]—dc20   93-11949   CIP   AC

"It's no use," said Mrs. Bear. "The baby won't go
to sleep."

"Mmmm?" said Mr. Bear.

"I can't take her with me to babysit for the Grizzly-Bears," said Mrs. Bear. "She'll keep them all awake . . ."

"Mmmm-hmm," said Mr. Bear.

"So you'll have to babysit instead," said Mrs. Bear.

"Mmmm," said Mr. Bear. "WHAT?"

Mr. Bear walked through the woods to the Grizzly-Bears' house and knocked on the door. Before he could say "I've come to babysit," a baby bear was thrust into his arms.

"We're late, we're very late," said Mr. and Mrs. Grizzly-Bear as they bolted out of the door.

Mr. Bear felt his arms getting sticky.

"You'll have to give the baby a bath," said a small bear who appeared at the end of the hall.

Mr. Bear didn't know how to bathe a baby. His wife always took care of that.

"You're not very good at that," said Fred as Mr. Bear drenched himself in the bathwater.

"That's not the right way to do it," said Ted as Mr. Bear tried to dry himself and the baby with the bathroom rug.

"I don't think you're a real babysitter," said Fuzz as the baby started to cry.

Mr. Bear didn't know how to stop babies from crying, so he patted the baby's head.

"You're not very good at that," said Fred as Mr. Bear rocked the baby up and down.

"That's not the right way to do it," said Ted as Mr. Bear tried to sing a lullaby.

> *"Twinkle, twinkle, little slug,*
> *Leaving slime trails on the rug . . ."*

"I don't think you're a real babysitter,"
said Fuzz as the baby went on crying.
  "Perhaps the baby's hungry," said Mr. Bear.
And he headed toward the kitchen.

Fred, Ted, and Fuzz watched Mr. Bear prepare a meal of raw fish. The baby wouldn't eat it.

"You're not very good at that," said Fred.

Then Mr. Bear offered some acorn mush. The baby spit it out.

"Don't you know that babies only eat honey? I'm *sure* you're not a real babysitter," said Fuzz.

So Mr. Bear carefully gave the baby some honey.

The baby's eyes began to close.

"It's very peaceful now," sighed Mr. Bear
as he settled down into a comfortable chair.
"I wonder what the others are doing?"

BONGA BONGA TWANGGG CRRRASHHH

The baby woke up and began to cry again.

"We were playing hide-and-seek," said Fred.

". . . but Fuzz hid in the clock," said Ted.

". . . and it wobbled too far," said Fuzz.

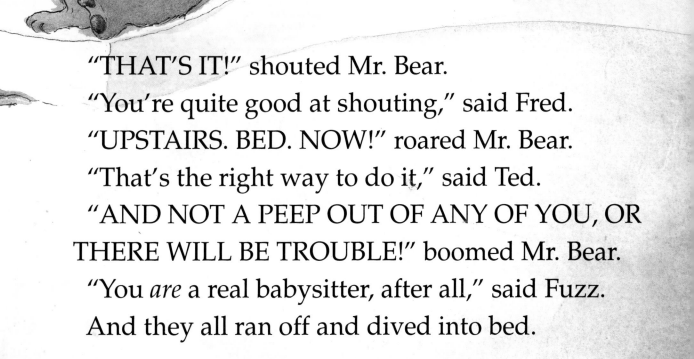

"THAT'S IT!" shouted Mr. Bear.

"You're quite good at shouting," said Fred.

"UPSTAIRS. BED. NOW!" roared Mr. Bear.

"That's the right way to do it," said Ted.

"AND NOT A PEEP OUT OF ANY OF YOU, OR THERE WILL BE TROUBLE!" boomed Mr. Bear.

"You *are* a real babysitter, after all," said Fuzz.

And they all ran off and dived into bed.

Mr. Bear and the baby went into the bathroom.
Mr. Bear washed and brushed the baby perfectly.
Mr. Bear and the baby went into the kitchen.

Mr. Bear cleaned up the mess, made himself a cup of tea, loaded a plate with cookies, and warmed a little honey, all the while humming a soothing lullaby to keep the baby happy.

Then Mr. Bear and the baby sank into the comfy chair in front of the fire, and very soon all was quiet.

Mr. Bear was just falling asleep when the Grizzly-Bears returned home.

"Don't know *how* you got that baby to sleep," said Mrs. Grizzly-Bear. "I always let my husband take care of that."

Mr. Bear smiled a secret smile to himself.

Mr. Bear walked home by moonlight past burrows and nests, where babies and children were being tucked in and lights were turned low for the night.

Mr. Bear's secret smile grew wider.

When he reached his house, Mr. Bear could hear his
baby crying.
Mr. Bear tiptoed inside.

"Can I help?" he asked.
"Yes. You could hold
her for a minute while I
make us both a cup of
blueberry tea," said Mrs. Bear.

Mr. Bear held his baby carefully in his lap and sang her a lullaby.

Her cries turned to little hiccupy sobs, and then to hiccups, and finally, with a small burp, she closed her eyes.

When Mrs. Bear brought the tea, she found Mr. Bear and his baby fast asleep.